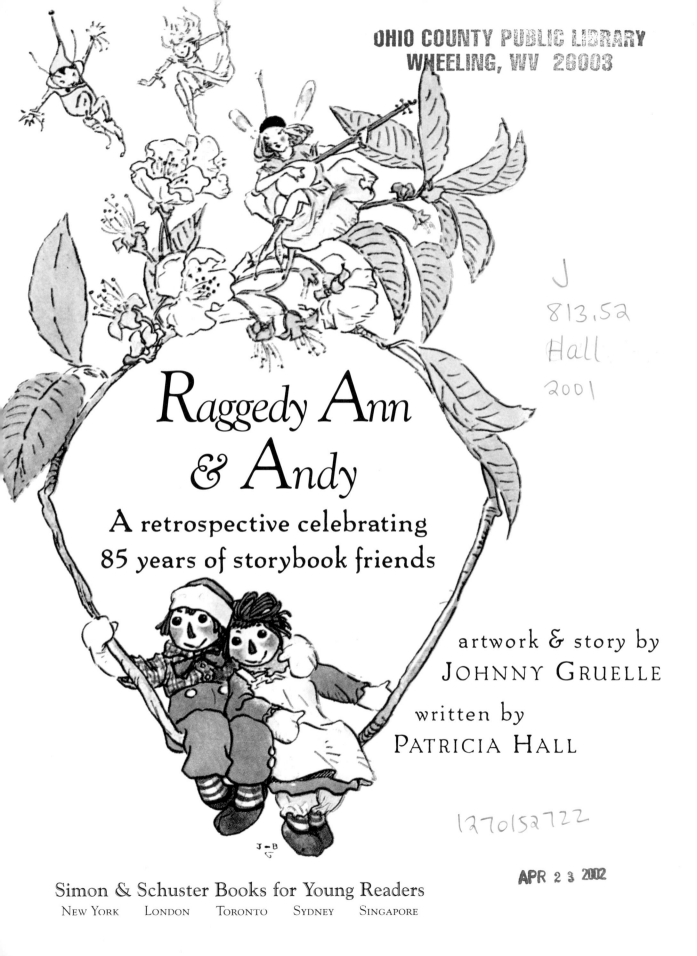

Raggedy Ann & Andy

A retrospective celebrating 85 years of storybook friends

artwork & story by
JOHNNY GRUELLE

written by
PATRICIA HALL

Simon & Schuster Books for Young Readers
NEW YORK   LONDON   TORONTO   SYDNEY   SINGAPORE

SIMON & SCHUSTER BOOKS FOR YOUNG READERS
An imprint of Simon & Schuster Children's Publishing Division
1230 Avenue of the Americas, New York, New York 10020

SIMON & SCHUSTER BOOKS FOR YOUNG READERS
is a trademark of Simon & Schuster.
Book design by Jennifer Reyes
The text for "Raggedy Ann's New Sisters" is set in Caslon Old Face BT.
The text for *Raggedy Ann and Andy: Celebrating 85 Years of
Storybook Friends* is set in Goudy Old Face.
Printed in Hong Kong
2 4 6 8 10 9 7 5 3 1
Library of Congress Cataloging-in-Publication Data
Hall, Patricia, 1948–
*Raggedy Ann and Andy: Celebrating 85 Years
of Storybook Friends* / creator, Johnny Gruelle ;
tribute by Patricia Hall.—1st ed.
p. cm.
Includes the story, Raggedy Ann's new sisters.
ISBN 0-689-84336-4
1. Gruelle, Johnny, 1880–1938—Characters—Raggedy Ann—Juvenile literature.
2. Gruelle, Johnny, 1880–1938—Characters—Raggedy Andy—Juvenile literature.
3. Children's stories, American—History and criticism—Juvenile literature.
4. Raggedy Ann (Fictitious character)—Juvenile literature. 5. Raggedy Andy (Fictitious
character) Juvenile literature. [1. Gruelle, Johnny, 1880–1938.
2. Raggedy Ann (Fictitious character). 3. Raggedy Andy (Fictitious character)]
I. Gruelle, Johnny, 1880–1938. II. Title.
PS3513.R874 Z69 2001
813'.52—dc 21   00-046398

For Kimberly, Katie,
and Kristina

Foreword

Although I never knew him, my childhood was surrounded with the love and laughter of Johnny Gruelle. Both his life and his magical creations came alive through the words of my grandmother Myrtle and my parents Worth and Sue as they read his stories to me each night at bedtime. How exciting it was for a little girl to learn that her very own grandfather had given the world so many wonderful characters. From my earliest years, my family included Raggedy Ann and Andy, the Camel with the Wrinkled Knees, Beloved Belindy, Snoopwiggy, and a host of other charming little critters. Thanks to my grandfather I was even able to journey through the heavens to the Magical Land of Noom.

Later on, I learned that Johnny was a very diverse and complex man. Although he is best known for creating the lovable and famous rag dolls known as Raggedy Ann and Andy, he was also a freelance artist, cartoonist, book illustrator, and businessman. Around 1908 he began producing features for children. When his daughter, Marcella, became ill and was bedridden, he spent many hours telling stories to entertain her. Sadly, Marcella died at the age of thirteen, but these stories, which were based on Marcella's own dolls and playtime activities, became the genesis for Johnny's illustrations and children's books.

There have been many accounts regarding the origins of the first Raggedy Ann doll. The most probable explanation was given in the early 1950s by Johnny's widow, Myrtle. She spoke of an old handmade rag doll made in Illinois many years before for Alice Benton, Myrtle's mother-in-law. This doll was found years later and, after a little repair work, became a new playmate for Marcella. The first commercial Raggedy Ann was patented on September 7, 1915, and Johnny Gruelle continued to write the Raggedy adventures as a tribute to Marcella until his death in 1938.

Today, Johnny's magic is still alive in the hearts of children of all ages. What an honor it has been for my husband, Tom, and me to commemorate his life and works through the official Johnny Gruelle Raggedy Ann and Andy Museum located in his birthplace, Arcola, Illinois. We believe deeply in my grandfather's philosophy of unconditional love and universal acceptance. It is our hope that many more generations will come to know and love the whimsical imagination of Johnny Gruelle.

I know that you will enjoy this glimpse of Johnny's world through the eyes of my special friend Patricia Hall.

Joni Gruelle Wannamaker

Joni Gruelle Wannamaker
Granddaughter, artist,
and co-founder of The Raggedy Ann Museum

A singing heart no sadness knows—gloom cannot start where gladness glows.
                              —RAGGEDY ANN

Peering down from atop a shelf, heads bent to one side, they could have been tossed up there yesterday. But the knowing smiles, wise shoe-button eyes, and smudges left from countless hugs and kisses give away the true age of these little playthings. If only these dolls could talk, what a tale they could tell—one that goes back more than eighty years.

Most everyone knows Raggedy Ann and Andy. Frolicking their way through adventure after adventure, the little rag dolls with the triangle noses and yarn hair have become worldwide symbols of love, friendship, and make-believe. Beloved by both children and adults, the venerable Raggedys that appear to have sprung from the mists of folk tradition are actually the inspired brainchildren of a turn-of-the-century artist named Johnny Gruelle, who got a bright idea from an old family plaything and decided to make something of it.

Johnny Gruelle—author, illustator, and toy designer. (*Courtesy Jane Gruelle Comerford*)

Born in 1880 in Arcola, Illinois, John Barton Gruelle spent his youth and young adulthood in the Midwest. An avid doodler all his life, Gruelle went to work as a newspaper cartoonist in Indianapolis at age nineteen, eventually moving to the New York area in 1910 to work as a freelance artist. There, fulfilling multiple assignments for newspapers and magazines, he refined his artistry and waited for his big break.

A political cartoonist as well as a comic artist, Gruelle stayed attentive to the world around him—an ever-evolving panorama of scientific invention, industrialization, and social change. He was particularly fascinated with watching people embrace the trappings of modern times while they steadfastly clung to safe reminders of a simpler past. Gruelle crafted his works accordingly, turning out comics and stories for readers being nudged by both the old-timey and the modern.

Gruelle's newspapers artistry ranged from portraits of
well-knowns such as Mark Twain to cartoon commentaries.

Shortly before relocating to the East Coast, Gruelle and his wife, Myrtle, had visited his parents in Indianapolis, where he'd stumbled upon an old homemade rag doll in the attic. Intrigued, Gruelle penned a new face on the age-worn doll. Inspired by two James Whitcomb Riley poems ("The Raggedy Man" and "Little Orphant Annie"), Gruelle christened the refurbished doll "Raggedy Ann," later presenting it to his young daughter, Marcella. Watching Marcella play, Gruelle began including little girls and their rag dolls in his comics—colorful picture-stories in which he deftly blended modern details with traditional themes and images.

Marcella Delight Gruelle *(Courtesy Worth and Sue Gruelle)*

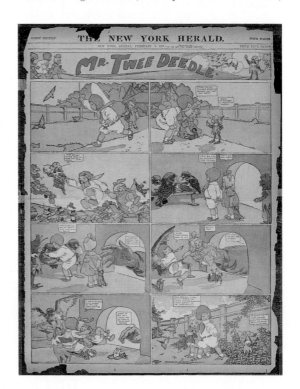

Gruelle's "Mr. Twee Deedle" comic page appeared every Sunday in the *New York Herald,* from 1911–1918.

In 1915, impressed by the burgeoning market for dolls based on comic characters, Johnny Gruelle sent off a hand-drawn design to the U.S. Patent Office for a character creation all his own. The folksy, friendly-looking doll was a stylized version of his daughter's own Raggedy Ann. Gruelle's entrepreneurial plan became clear as he and his family fabricated a number of handmade Raggedy Ann dolls to sell through interstate commerce—enough to qualify for a trademark for the name and logo "Raggedy Ann." Although no one has verified how many (or how few) of these first dolls were produced, Gruelle most likely used some of them as prototypes to pique the interest of a commercial company.

UNITED STATES PATENT OFFICE.

JOHN B. GRUELLE, OF NEW YORK, N. Y.

DESIGN FOR A DOLL.

47,789.   Specification for Design.   Patented Sept. 7, 1915.

Application filed May 28, 1915. Serial No. 31,073. Term of patent 14 years.

To all whom it may concern:

Be it known that I, JOHN B. GRUELLE, a citizen of the United States, residing at New York city, in the county of New York and State of New York, have invented a new, original, and ornamental Design for a Doll, of which the following is a specification, reference being had to the accompanying drawings, forming part thereof.

Figures 1 and 2 are front and side elevations respectively of a doll, showing my new design.

I claim:

The ornamental design for a doll, as shown.

JOHN B. GRUELLE.

Copies of this patent may be obtained for five cents each, by addressing the "Commissioner of Patents, Washington, D. C."

DESIGN.
J. B. GRUELLE.
DOLL.
APPLICATION FILED MAY 28, 1915.

47,789.   Patented Sept. 7, 1915.

Fig. 2.   *Fig. 1.*

During that same summer, Gruelle successfully pitched an idea for a rag-doll storybook to the P. F. Volland Company of Chicago. However, three years would pass before children would meet Raggedy Ann. For as Johnny Gruelle was about to taste the fruits of his effort, he experienced the greatest of all losses. His daughter, Marcella, who suffered from valvular heart disease, fell ill from an unsterile vaccination. Despite medical attention and prolonged bed rest, her condition steadily worsened, and on November 8, 1915, Marcella Gruelle passed away at age thirteen.

Grieving for his daughter but needing to work, Johnny Gruelle stayed at his drawing board, turning out newspaper comic pages, magazine stories, and book illustration commissions. He also finished the collection of tales he had promised the Volland Company—ones he had made up for Marcella, about the adventures of a doll named Raggedy Ann.

Marcella Gruelle drawn by her father, 1912
(*Courtesy Worth and Sue Gruelle*)

In September 1918 the Volland Company published Gruelle's *Raggedy Ann Stories.* It was the first in what would be a series of more than two dozen storybooks, published during and after Gruelle's lifetime. Intertwining history with embellishment, Gruelle's introduction to *Raggedy Ann Stories* tells of how a long-forgotten family doll was discovered in Grandmother's attic—not by a grown man, but by a little girl named Marcella.

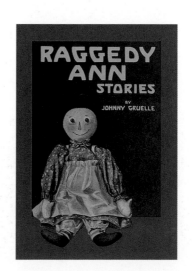

U̲nderlying all of the tales in *Raggedy Ann Stories* was a basic theme that would provide the foundation for all subsequent Raggedy books; namely, that dolls and toys come to life when the humans are away. Once the

coast was clear, playthings could transform into walking, talking, giggling personalities, able to play, cook up schemes, even escape out the nursery window to lands of make-believe.

Gruelle took great care in presenting his Raggedy Ann character, costuming her in nostalgic nineteenth-century-style clothing befitting a doll

who had lain hidden in an attic trunk for fifty years. He also gave her a double-edged persona. Silent and enigmatic whenever people were present, Raggedy Ann became an animated, spirited leader of the dolls once the humans were elsewhere.

The final tale in *Raggedy Ann Stories*, entitled "Raggedy Ann's New Sisters," tells of Marcella's Raggedy Ann being taken far away to be used as a model for dozens of identical factory-made dolls. This charming finale is a storybook version of a real-life event. By the time the first copies of *Raggedy Ann Stories* were rolling off the presses, the P. F. Volland Company was already receiving shipments of dozens of manufactured Raggedy Ann dolls—ones that

Volland "Book House" at
Marshall Field's department store, 1929.

had intentionally been patterned after Gruelle's book illustrations and authorized by Gruelle to be sold by Volland.

When introduced to the retail market in late 1918, the book-doll combination was a hit. Children were enchanted with a doll they could hug and also read stories about. Merchants were delighted to offer both products together. And the Volland Company soon had other Raggedy products, including an entire line of valentines, ready to sell. In engineering such a scenario, Gruelle and the

Montgomery Ward catalogue, 1929

Volland Company were among the early pioneers of what has today become a multibillion-dollar industry—character merchandising.

Another tale in *Raggedy Ann Stories*, entitled "Raggedy Ann and the Painter," introduces little readers to something extra special, nestled deep inside Raggedy Ann's white cotton stuffing—a candy heart. In giving his storybook doll a heart, Gruelle (either unwittingly or with the sense of humor for which he was known) launched a tenacious legend that would be repeated again and again as factual history: that the first Raggedy Ann doll prototypes made by the Gruelle family in 1915 possessed actual candy hearts with "I Love You" printed on them.

This small cardboard heart was sewn inside early Volland Company Raggedy Anns.

Putting actual sugar hearts in real-life dolls suited Gruelle's inventive nature, and it is conceivable that he and his family did place sweets inside the first few dolls they produced. Gruelle's son Worth, though quite young at the time, recalled being sent to the candy store to fetch the sugar hearts that were later stuffed into the chest of each doll. Moreover, many faithful fans and collectors continue to believe that the original Raggedy Ann dolls did, in fact, possess hearts of candy, although none has ever been documented. More important, perhaps, than the factual or fictional nature of the candy heart legend is its charm and power to provide Raggedy Ann with an authentic source for her storybook sweetness.

Myrtle and Johnny's sons Richard and Worth, as
young children. (*Courtesy Margaret Gruelle Owen*)

The success of Raggedy Ann spurred Gruelle to create a brother for her, and in 1920 Raggedy Andy was introduced as a doll and in his own book of tales. *Raggedy Andy Stories* continued the make-believe adventures in Marcella's nursery, explaining in its own opening pages how Raggedy Andy happened to arrive one day, all rolled up in a package addressed to Johnny Gruelle, otherwise known as Daddy.

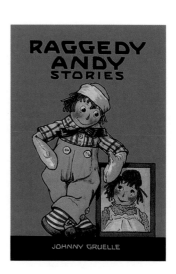

Gruelle portrayed Raggedy Andy as a classic little boy. Exuberant and lively, Andy quickly carves out his own special niche, charming the other dolls and inventing new kinds of mischief. Even without

a candy heart, Raggedy Andy exudes an amiable personality, proving that little boys can be both boyish and kind.

Like a typical brother and sister, Raggedy Ann and Raggedy Andy conspire together on shenanigans, concoct childlike rationales for the puzzling details of everyday life, and extricate each other from a variety of minor mishaps, sometimes losing a bit of stuffing in the process. Being the older (and therefore wiser) sibling, Raggedy Ann usually has the last word, and like little brothers everywhere, Raggedy Andy sometimes sulks. But this range of attributes and behaviors makes the dolls strong, believable role models for little readers of both sexes.

Standing careful watch over the nursery *Raggedy Ann Stories* and *Raggedy Andy Stories* is a character named Marcella—a charming human protagonist named after Gruelle's own late daughter. The storybook Marcella embodies the interests, dreams, and activities of an idealized little girl. Innocent and playful, she hosts tea parties, tucks her playthings in at night, and explains things in great detail to her dolls, as though they were human

(never suspecting that they might be thinking their *own* thoughts). The Marcella character would appear again in several subsequent Raggedy books, and in 1929 Gruelle would honor his daughter with a full volume of tales entitled *Marcella: A Raggedy Ann Story.*

Johnny Gruelle continued adding to a growing list of Raggedy

Ann and Andy books during the 1920s and early 1930s—books that garnered

a solid following among children, parents, and classroom teachers. Each new

volume of adventures was filled with fanciful themes and images, many

inspired by Gruelle's wistful recollections of his own Midwest childhood. As he

wrote, Gruelle introduced new characters—an eclectic array of dolls, stuffed

animals, cuddly puppies, and forest and meadow critters who join the Raggedys,

at different times, as companions, coconspirators, and helpers who offer

guidance and assistance.

Gruelle set many Raggedy tales in the safe and comfy confines of Marcella's nursery, a sunlit haven in which readers can easily suspend their disbelief and become a part of the make-believe. Many of the Raggedy friends included dolls such as the kilted Scots doll Uncle Clem and the blue-uniformed Percy Policeman, each resembling a German Steiff doll. There is also the maternal Beloved Belindy, patterned after a plump African-American mammy doll, as well as the Dutch dolls Henny and Frederika, and the stuffed animals Little Brown Bear, Sunny Bunny, and Eddie Elephant.

Sometimes the nursery serves as a jumping-off place for more enchanted destinations. The Deep Deep Woods and the Golden Meadow are leafy, friendly places, inspired by the Connecticut countryside where Gruelle lived. Slipping out the window after everyone is asleep, Raggedy Ann and Andy love escaping to these open-air fairylands where magical things can— and usually do—happen. Here they meet up with comrades like the Camel with the Wrinkled Knees (who "wabbled" about on unsteady, crumpled legs) and are greeted by witches and wizards, gossamer-winged fairies, and Lilliputian forest people who peek out from behind

mushrooms. The thatched cottages, sunny pathways, and babbling brooks are perfect for the impromptu journeys and exciting searches and rescues that usually conclude with the Raggedys returning safely to their beds in the nursery before the real-life folks awaken.

SUNNY BUNNY, LITTLE BROWN BEAR,
RAGGEDY ANN, EDDIE ELEPHANT, HENNY

WOODEN WILLIE

MISTER MINKY

BELOVED BELINDY

FREDERIKA AND RAGGEDY ANN

HOOKIE THE GOBLIN

(CLOCKWISE FROM TOP) CLEETY THE CLOWN,
UNCLE CLEM, RAGGEDY ANDY, RAGGEDY ANN,
SQUEAKIE, BELOVED BELINDY, ROSA, AND
THE FRENCH DOLL, A TEDDY BEAR
AND QUACKY DOODLES

RAGGEDY ANN AND FIDO

CLEETY THE CLOWN

FREDDY FOX AND BERTRAM BEAR

THE GEEWHILIKER, GURGLE GLUG, FUZZYWUMP

Storybook Friends ♥

THE CAMEL WITH THE WRINKLED KNEES
AND THE TIRED OLD HORSE

PERCY POLICEMAN

THE SNITZNOODLE

(FROM TOP) FOREST CRITTERS, RAGGEDY ANDY, RAGGEDY ANN,
GRINNY BEAR, SNOOPYWIGGY, AND WIGGYSNOOP

EDDIE ELF

RAGGEDY ANDY AND LITTLE WEAKIE

Gruelle crafted his Raggedy stories so that all children could participate in the adventures. Whether having tea in the nursery, tumbling head over heels down a magical slippery slide, or exploring the Deep Deep Woods, youngsters can feel like they are right there, holding the hands of the rag dolls. At its best when read aloud, Gruelle's unpretentious prose unfolds at a leisurely pace, told the way a child might tell it, employing simple language and syntax. Frequent literary detours give the stories a distinct charm and allow for the full blossoming of Gruelle's storybook magic. The deliciously drawn-out plots invite children to relish the story line and anticipate the climax.

Using the logic and phrasing of children, Gruelle filled his stories with alliterative and rhythmic modifiers ("frowningest frown," "real-for-sure"), ingenuous phrases ("nice red shiny bicycle"), and evocative terminology ("blump," for the sound a rag doll makes when it hits the floor). The Raggedys and their friends take liberties in their use of the English language, holding forth with amusing, childlike malapropisms. This quirky vernacular allows little readers and listeners to embrace the Raggedy tales on, quite literally, their own terms.

Like all good fairy tales, the Raggedy stories incorporate numerous mouthwatering edibles (multiflavored soda fountains, luscious lollipop gardens, and ever-replenishing cream puffs), magical metamorphoses (characters changing from commoner to royalty, from obstinate to well behaved); and enchanted objects (wishing pebbles and left-handed safety pins, to name only a few).

Each Raggedy story builds upon one or more moral messages. Never heavy-handed or overbearing, virtues such as optimism, compassion, tolerance, diversity, loyalty, inclusion, and acceptance are interwoven in the fabric of the Raggedy tales in the form of gentle lessons, usually taught by the two very ethical rag dolls.

Accompanying the fanciful prose in the Raggedy Ann and Andy books were Gruelle's colorful, dynamic illustrations. Influenced by his father—Hoosier Group fine artist R. B. Gruelle—as well as other late-nineteenth- and early-twentieth-century illustrators, such as Arthur Rackham and Howard Pyle, Johnny Gruelle developed an artistic style distinctly his own. His illustrations in the first several Raggedy books were impressionistic,

softly colored renditions of three-dimensional dolls and toys going about their storybook business. Commenting on Gruelle's early artistic style, Professor Jack Zipes has noted, "Gruelle contrasted the figures of good and evil in his line drawings in a way that induced an atmosphere of hope. For Gruelle, a fairy-tale illustration always had to point to the possibility of attaining a happy end."*

*Jack Zipes, trans., "A Note on the Illustrations," in *The Complete Fairy Tales of the Brothers Grimm* (New York: Bantam Books, 1987).

As time went on, Gruelle simplified his illustrations, depicting his Raggedys with bolder, more defined lines and splashes of vibrant color. He had a flair for capturing playthings in motion, as they slid down a rainspout, hung upside down on a line to dry, or lay doubled over in a humorous heap. It was as though he truly knew what it was like to be inside a doll's body, doing doll things. Throughout his career Gruelle drew the Raggedys many different ways, but he always retained his singular knack for capturing the dolls' puckish expressions, inimitable gestures, and irrepressible personalities. After Gruelle's death in 1938 his brother, Justin, and son Worth carried on this tradition, each illustrating several Raggedy Ann books in Johnny's own charming style.

So now, more than eighty years since they first sprang to life, Johnny Gruelle's little rag dolls find themselves standing on the brink of a new century. Amazingly, while dozens of other storybook characters have emerged, then faded into obscurity, the unabashedly old-fashioned Raggedys have remained popular, proving themselves again and again as timeless role models. Despite social changes and shifts in child-rearing philosophies, the Raggedy stories continue to resonate as positive allegories for young children, not to mention the grown-ups who grew up with the tales and are delighted to pass along the tradition. "Raggedy Ann and Andy are cultural icons, as American as apple pie and Uncle Sam," notes Dee Jones, Curator of the de Grummond Collection at the University of Mississippi. Currently serving on the Caldecott Committee for the American Library Association, Jones notes the timeless quality of Gruelle's prose and illustrations. She adds, "Though Raggedy Ann and Andy originally sparked the imagination of a nation recovering from World War I, new generations of children continue to derive pleasure and comfort from Gruelle's loveable storybook characters."

When Johnny Gruelle sat down nearly a century ago to create Raggedy Ann, he envisioned a nostalgic character that would appeal to a modern audience. Ever since, Raggedy Ann and Andy have continued to evoke a past time—if only in our imaginations—when life seemed kinder, sweeter, and less complicated. Whether trekking through the Deep Deep Woods or minding their manners at a doll tea party, Raggedy Ann and Andy carry on, reminding us to delight in simple pleasures, hold fast to the magic, and never forget that true happiness always comes from within.

The ever-huggable Raggedys continue to delight children.
(Photo by Pat Casey Daley)

RAGGEDY ANN'S NEW SISTERS

A TALE FROM RAGGEDY ANN STORIES

WRITTEN & ILLUSTRATED BY
JOHNNY GRUELLE

Raggedy Ann's New Sisters

Marcella was having a tea party up in the nursery when Daddy called to her, so she left the dollies sitting around the tiny table and ran down stairs carrying Raggedy Ann with her.

Mama, Daddy and a strange man were talking in the living room and Daddy introduced Marcella to the stranger.

The stranger was a large man with kindly eyes and a cheery smile, as pleasant as Raggedy Ann's.

He took Marcella upon his knee and ran his fingers through her curls as he talked to Daddy and Mama, so, of course, Raggedy Ann liked him from the beginning. "I have two little girls," he told Marcella. "Their names are Virginia and Doris, and one time when we were at the sea-shore they were playing in the sand and they covered up Freddy, Doris' boy-doll in the sand. They were playing that Freddy was in bathing and that he wanted to be covered with the clean white sand, just as the other bathers did. And when they had covered Freddy they took their little pails and shovels and went farther down the beach to play and forgot all about Freddy.

"Now when it came time for us to go home, Virginia and Doris remembered Freddy and ran down to get him, but the tide had come in and Freddy was 'way out under the water and they could not find him. Virginia and Doris were very sad and they talked of Freddy all the way home."

"It was too bad they forgot Freddy," said Marcella.

"Yes, indeed it was!" the new friend replied as he took Raggedy Ann up and made her dance on Marcella's knee. "But it turned out all right after all, for do you know what happened to Freddy?"

"No, what did happen to him?" Marcella asked.

"Well, first of all, when Freddy was covered with the sand, he enjoyed it immensely. And he did not mind it so much when the tide came up over him, for he felt Virginia and Doris would return and get him.

"But presently Freddy felt the sand above him move as if someone was digging him out. Soon his head was uncovered and he could look right up through the pretty green water, and what do you think was happening? The Tide Fairies were uncovering Freddy!

"When he was completely uncovered, the Tide Fairies swam with Freddy 'way out to the Undertow Fairies. The Undertow Fairies took Freddy and swam with him 'way out to the Roller Fairies. The Roller Fairies carried Freddy up to the surface and tossed him up to the Spray Fairies who carried him to the Wind Fairies."

"And the Wind Fairies?" Marcella asked breathlessly.

"The Wind Fairies carried Freddy right to our garden and there Virginia and Doris found him, none the worse for his wonderful adventure!"

"Freddy must have enjoyed it and your little girls must have been very glad to get Freddy back again!" said Marcella. "Raggedy Ann went up in the air on the tail of a kite one day and fell and was lost, so now I am very careful with her!"

"Would you let me take Raggedy Ann for a few days?" asked the new friend.

Marcella was silent. She liked the stranger friend, but she did not wish to lose Raggedy Ann.

"I will promise to take very good care of her and return her to you in a week. Will you let her go with me, Marcella?"

Marcella finally agreed and when the stranger friend left, he placed Raggedy Ann in his grip.

"It is lonely without Raggedy Ann!" said the dollies each night.

"We miss her happy painted smile and her cheery ways!" they said.

And so the week dragged by. . . .

But, my! What a chatter there was in the nursery the first night after Raggedy Ann returned. All the dolls were so anxious to hug Raggedy Ann they could scarcely wait until Marcella had left them alone.

When they had squeezed Raggedy Ann almost out of shape and she had smoothed out her yarn hair, patted her apron out and felt her shoe-button eyes to see if they were still there, she said, "Well, what have you been doing? Tell me all the news!"

"Oh we have just had the usual tea parties and games!" said the tin soldier. "Tell us about yourself, Raggedy dear, we have missed you so much!"

"Yes! Tell us where you have been and what you have done, Raggedy!" all the dolls cried.

But Raggedy Ann just then noticed that one of the penny dolls had a hand missing.

"How did this happen?" she asked as she picked up the doll.

"I fell off the table and lit upon the tin soldier last night when we were playing. But don't mind a little thing like that, Raggedy Ann," replied the penny doll. "Tell us of yourself! Have you had a nice time?"

"I shall not tell a thing until your hand is mended!" Raggedy Ann said.

So the Indian ran and brought a bottle of glue. "Where's the hand?" Raggedy asked.

"In my pocket," the penny doll answered.

When Raggedy Ann had glued the penny doll's hand in place and wrapped a rag around it to hold it until the glue dried, she said, "When I tell you of this wonderful adventure, I know you will all feel very happy. It has made me almost burst my stitches with joy."

The dolls all sat upon the floor around Raggedy Ann, the tin soldier with his arm over her shoulder.

"Well, first when I left," said Raggedy Ann, "I was placed in the Stranger Friend's grip. It was rather stuffy in there, but I did not mind it; in fact I believe I must have fallen asleep, for when I awakened I saw the Stranger Friend's hand reaching into the grip. Then he lifted me from the grip and danced me upon his knee. 'What do you think of her?' he asked to three other men sitting nearby.

"I was so interested in looking out of the window I did not pay any attention to what they said, for we were on a train and the scenery was just flying by! Then I was put back in the grip.

"When next I was taken from the grip I was in a large, clean, light room and there were many, many girls all dressed in white aprons.

"The Stranger Friend showed me to another man and to the girls who took off my clothes, cut my seams and took out my cotton. And what do you think! They found my lovely candy heart had not melted at all as I thought. Then they laid me on a table and marked all around my outside edges with a pencil on clean white cloth, and then the girls re-stuffed me and dressed me.

"I stayed in the clean big light room for two or three days and nights and watched my sisters grow from pieces of cloth into rag dolls just like myself!"

"Your SISTERS!" the dolls all exclaimed in astonishment. "What do you mean, Raggedy?"

"I mean," said Raggedy Ann, "that the Stranger Friend had borrowed me from Marcella so that he could have patterns made from me. And before I left the big clean white room there were hundreds of rag dolls so like me you would not have been able to tell us apart."

"We could have told *you* by your happy smile!" cried the French dolly.

"But all of my sister dolls have smiles just like mine!" replied Raggedy Ann.

"And shoe-button eyes?" the dolls all asked.

"Yes, shoe-button eyes!" Raggedy Ann replied.

"I would tell you from the others by your dress, Raggedy Ann," said the French doll. "Your dress is fifty years old! I could tell you by that!"

"But my new sister rag dolls have dresses just like mine, for the Stranger Friend had cloth made especially for them exactly like mine."

"I know how we could tell you from the other rag dolls, even if you all look exactly alike!" said the Indian doll, who had been thinking for a long time.

"How?" asked Raggedy Ann with a laugh.

"By feeling your candy heart! If the doll has a candy heart then it is you, Raggedy Ann!"

Raggedy Ann laughed, "I am so glad you all love me as you do, but I am sure you would not be able to tell me from my new sisters, except that I am more worn, for each new rag doll has a candy heart, and on it is written, '*I love you*' just as is written on my own candy heart."

"And there are hundreds and hundreds of the new rag dolls?" asked the little penny dolls.

"Hundreds and hundreds of them, all named Raggedy Ann," replied Raggedy.

"Then," said the penny dolls, "we are indeed happy and proud for you! For wherever one of the new Raggedy Ann dolls goes there will go with it the love and happiness that *you* give to others."

Johnny Gruelle's Raggedy Ann and Andy Books

Raggedy Ann Stories (1918)

Raggedy Andy Stories (1920)

Raggedy Ann and Andy and the Camel with the Wrinkled Knees (1924)

Raggedy Andy's Number Book (1924)

Raggedy Ann's Wishing Pebble (1925)

Raggedy Ann's Alphabet Book (1925)

Beloved Belindy (1926)

The Paper Dragon (1926)

Wooden Willie (1927)

Raggedy Ann's Magical Wishes (1928)

Marcella: A Raggedy Ann Story (1929)

Raggedy Ann in the Deep Deep Woods (1930)

Raggedy Ann's Sunny Songs (1930)

Raggedy Ann in Cookie Land (1931)

Raggedy Ann's Lucky Pennies (1932)

Raggedy Ann and the Left-Handed Safety Pin (1935)

Raggedy Ann Cut-out Paper Doll (1935)

Raggedy Ann in the Golden Meadow (1935)

Raggedy Ann's Joyful Songs (1937)

Raggedy Ann and Maizie Moocow (1937)

Raggedy Ann in the Magic Book (1939)

Raggedy Ann and the Golden Butterfly (1940)

Raggedy Ann and Andy and the Nice Fat Policeman (1942)

Raggedy Ann and Betsy Bonnet String (1943)

Raggedy Ann in the Snow White Castle (1946)

Raggedy Ann and the Golden Ring (1961)

Raggedy Ann and the Happy Meadow (1961)

Raggedy Ann and the Hobby Horse (1961)

Raggedy Ann and the Wonderful Witch (1961)